I am an ARO PUBLISHING TEN WORD BOOK

My ten words are:

bounce   runs

pass   jumps

the   shoots

ball   slam

he   dunk

SLAM DUNK

10 WORDS

Story and Pictures by
Bob Reese

4-98

©1995 by ARO Publishing Co. All rights reserved, including the right of reproduction in whole or in part in any form. Designed and produced by ARO Publishing Co. printed in the U.S.A. P.O. Box 193 Provo, Utah 84603
ISBN 0-89868-289-4—Library Bound
ISBN 0-89868-288-6—Soft Bound

Bounce, bounce, bounce.

He runs.

He passes
the ball.

He runs ...

He jumps ...

He shoots
the ball.